MAINE
IS A MILLION MILES AWAY

WENDY KESSELMAN

For Susan
Photographs by Norma Holt

Copyright © 1989, 1976 by Wendy Kesselman.
All rights reserved. Published by Scholastic Inc.
SPRINT and SPRINT BOOKS are trademarks of Scholastic Inc.
Printed in the U.S.A.
ISBN 0-590-35177-X

2 3 4 5 6 7 8 9 10   31   03 02 01 00 99 98 97 96

CHAPTER 1

Sarah got up early. The sun was shining through the flowered yellow curtains that her mother had made a year ago. Sarah loved them, and she loved her room. She also loved the apartment house she lived in, even though it was old and rundown. She had lived in it all her life.

Today Sarah felt happy. In a week her best friend, Susan, would be back from camp. Summer was ending. In two weeks school would begin.

Sarah had never liked school. There were too many kids, and there was too much noise. Sometimes there was so much noise that Sarah couldn't even hear the teacher. But being in the same class with Susan made everything seem better.

Sarah remembered the first time she ever saw Susan. Susan was fighting with Pete in the school yard. Her face was dirty. Her hair was wild. All the kids were watching. Susan put up a good fight, but she lost. The other kids went back to class, but Sarah stayed outside. She gave Susan her handkerchief.

"I hate that Pete," Sarah said. "He always spoils everything."

Susan smiled at her. "You never get into

fights, do you?" she said. "You are always off by yourself."

Sarah and Susan talked for a while. They were late to class. But they didn't care. From then on, they were friends.

Every day they walked to school together. They walked home together too. On weekdays they did homework together. And on Saturdays they went to the movies. Sarah could talk to Susan about anything. She could tell Susan things she had never told anyone else.

Sarah reached under her pillow. She took out a letter from Susan. Sarah had read it many times. Now she read it over again.

Dear Sarah,

Camp is great! Maybe next summer you can come too. I caught a big fish. We cooked it outside on the fire. I wish I could bring a piece home for you.

I think about you a lot. I'll be home on Friday night — just one week from today! I can't wait to see you. We can go to the park on Saturday.

I miss you.

Love,

Susan

CHAPTER 2

Sarah had just finished reading Susan's letter when her mother came in. "Sarah," she said, "your father and I have something to tell you. Come into the living room."

Sarah hated it when her mother used that tone of voice. She only used it when something was wrong.

In the living room, her mother and father exchanged a look. Sarah knew that look. It meant they had a secret. All of a sudden, she was afraid.

"Sit down, Sarah," said her father. "Your mother and I have made a decision. We want to talk to you about it."

"What is it?" Sarah asked.

"We are moving," said her father.

Sarah looked at him. She couldn't believe it. "But why? Where are we going?" she asked.

"Sarah, we have to move," said her father. "You know how hard it's been for me to find work. Well, my friend Paul is working in Maine. And he just got me a job there."

Sarah looked down. She felt numb. Maine! How could they? Maine was about a million miles away. What about Susan? How could they be friends if Sarah lived that far away? It would be impossible.

"Listen," her mother said. "There is a good school there. And we'll be able to live in the country. That will be nice."

Would it be nice? Sarah wondered. She felt as if nothing would ever be nice again.

"Say something to us, Sarah," her mother said. "Please."

Sarah saw how big her mother's eyes were. They always got that way when she was worried. Sarah tried to smile. "When are we leaving?" she asked.

"On Friday," said her father.

"But on Saturday I'm going to the park with Susan," cried Sarah. "She won't be back until Friday night."

Sarah's parents looked at each other.

"OK," said her father. "We'll leave Saturday night. Now, start thinking about all the new friends you're going to make in Maine."

Sarah looked at her parents. They just didn't understand. What if she did make new friends? She would never have another friend like Susan.

CHAPTER 3

That night Sarah had a bad dream. She dreamed that they couldn't find a place to stay in Maine. They came back to the city, but their apartment house had burned down. Sarah woke up crying. Her mother came into the room. She rocked Sarah in her arms.

"You will be happy in Maine, Sarah," she said. "You will be just as happy as you are here. It may take a little time. But you will see. Life will be better there. We won't have to worry as much about money."

"But what about our apartment, Mommy?" Sarah cried. "What about my room? I love it here. I don't want to go so far away."

"It will be beautiful there," her mother said. "You will love living in the country. You will be able to see horses and cows and deer all the time. Now go back to sleep. Tomorrow you will feel better. You will begin to get used to the idea of leaving."

Sarah lay awake for a long time after her mother had gone. She stared at the ceiling. She looked at the curtains her mother had made. Would they take them along? she wondered. Would they fit the new windows? She felt the warm summer breeze on her face. She had been happy in this room. No other room would ever be the same. She turned her face to the pillow. *No*, thought Sarah, *I will never get used to it.*

CHAPTER 4

It was Saturday — Sarah's last day in the city. It was the last time she would see Susan. It was the last morning she would be in her own room. Her clothes were packed, her books were in a box, and her pictures were off the wall. The yellow curtains were gone. The room looked empty.

Sarah closed her eyes. She tried to imagine waking up in another room. She tried to imagine going to another school and having another friend. But it seemed impossible.

The doorbell rang. It was Susan. She was brown from the sun, and her eyes were shining. "Sarah!" she cried. "I'm back!"

Sarah smiled too. But inside, she felt sad.

They walked to the park. Susan told Sarah all about her summer. She talked about fishing and diving and sleeping in a tent and riding in a canoe. She talked on and on.

"But Sarah," she finally asked. "Why are you so quiet?"

Sarah gulped. "I have something to tell you," she said. "But it's hard to say."

"What is it?" Susan asked. "Tell me."

"We are going away," Sarah said.

"Going away? But where? When?"

Sarah's eyes filled with tears. She looked

away. "Tonight," she said. "We're moving to Maine."

"Oh, no!" cried Susan. "But why are you moving? I won't let you go."

Sarah was trying not to cry. "It's my father," she said. "He couldn't find work here. But there is a job for him in Maine."

"But you can't go!" cried Susan. "Maine is a million miles away. Nothing will be the same without you. I'll be so lonely."

"So will I," Sarah said in a whisper.

They looked at each other. Then they looked ahead, down the path. "Hey!" said Susan. "We walked all the way to the merry-go-round!"

It was strange. They had not been on the merry-go-round since second grade. Sarah remembered one fall day when they had ridden round and round until it grew dark. Since then they had not gone back. They felt they were too old for it. But today it felt right.

Sarah chose a black horse, Susan a brown one. The music started. Round and round they went, up and down. They looked at each other and laughed. The trees spun by. The world spun by. Sarah wished the music would never stop. She wanted to ride on the merry-go-round with Susan forever. Getting off meant going home. And going home meant leaving the city. Sarah clung to the horse's neck. It was a race against loneliness.

CHAPTER 5

The sun was low in the sky when the girls left the park, but still they walked slowly.

"You'll be late," Susan said.

"I know," said Sarah. "But it doesn't matter. It was so much fun."

It did matter. Her mother and father were waiting. The car was all ready.

"Where were you?" asked Sarah's mother. "We've been waiting for over an hour." But then she looked at the two girls' faces and stopped.

"We were at the merry-go-round," said Sarah. But she was thinking about something else. She was thinking that this was her last moment with Susan.

Sarah hugged her friend tightly. "Good-bye, Susan," she said. "Write to me."

Susan's dark eyes seemed enormous. "I will," she promised. Then she took off her Statue-of-Liberty charm bracelet. She had bought it last year when the class visited the Statue. "Here, take this," said Susan, holding out the bracelet. "I can go there any old time, but you will be too far away."

Sarah took the bracelet. She smiled through her tears. "Good-bye," she said.

As they drove away, Sarah looked back. She could still see Susan, standing there.

CHAPTER 6

Maine was beautiful. Sarah loved the trees and the ocean and the rolling hills. But school was awful. All the kids knew each other, but no one knew Sarah. No one wanted to know her, either.

Sarah was walking to school. In her sweater pocket she felt a letter from Susan. It was chilly out, but the letter made Sarah feel warm. The bracelet Susan had given her hung from her wrist. Sarah wore it all the time.

"School is fun this year," Susan had written. "But it isn't the same without you." Sarah wished she could write that her school was fun too. But nothing about it seemed like fun to Sarah.

She walked into the classroom. The other kids looked at her coldly. "Sarah," said the teacher, "I was just saying that tomorrow I'd like all of you to bring something special to class. Something you can tell us a story about. Something you can share with us."

Sarah nodded. She thought she heard someone giggle. She felt as if the whole class was laughing at her. She walked to her seat without looking at anybody.

That day school seemed longer than ever. Sarah daydreamed and stared out the window. She couldn't think of a single thing to bring to class. What a silly idea, she said to herself. She was too old for such games.

There was a girl in the class today she had never seen. Her name was Julie. She had been out sick for two weeks. Every now and then Sarah noticed Julie looking at her. But each time Sarah looked away.

After school everybody crowded around Julie. She seemed to be everybody's friend. As usual, Sarah was all alone. "Who is that?" she heard Julie say.

"The new girl. She's from New York City," someone answered.

"She seems very quiet," said Julie.

"Very stuck-up, you mean." There were giggles. They were laughing at her again. Sarah walked away quickly. Her face was hot. She was not stuck-up. How could they say that? They were the ones who were stuck-up.

When she got home, she went straight to her room and slammed the door. It was a beautiful day, but Sarah didn't want to be outside. She took out Susan's letter, but she couldn't even look at it. Just thinking about Susan made her cry.

Sarah lay down on her bed. She decided that she wouldn't go to school tomorrow. She would say she was sick. She would never go back to that school. Let them laugh all they wanted to — she wouldn't be there to hear them. She was never going there again.

CHAPTER 7

"Sarah!" called her mother. "Come quick. I want to show you something."

"Later, Mom," Sarah called back.

"No, come now. You might miss it."

"OK," Sarah called. Slowly she got to her feet. "I'm coming."

Her mother was outside in the garden. She

was on her knees, looking at something. At first Sarah thought it was a cat or a dog.

"Look at them, Sarah," said her mother. "They are fantastic!"

Sarah looked again. She saw four funny little animals. Were they . . .? Raccoons! Sarah remembered seeing them in the zoo.

Sarah came closer. "Oh, they're so cute," she

said. Her mother was feeding them pieces of bread. "Can I feed them?" asked Sarah.

She held out a crust of bread, and one of the raccoons came right up and took it. The raccoon had little hands, almost like a child's.

"I saw them last night," said Sarah's mother. "But you had already gone to sleep."

Sarah started to pat one of the raccoons. "You'd better not," her mother said. "They might bite your hand if there's no food in it."

Sarah and her mother sat with the raccoons until it got dark. Sarah loved their funny faces. The dark patches around their eyes made them look like robbers wearing masks.

"Do we have to go in?" Sarah asked when her mother stood up.

"We'll be having dinner soon, Sarah. And you must have homework to do for school."

Sarah frowned. She had managed to forget about school for a little while, but now her mother had reminded her.

Sarah's mother looked at her. "What's wrong?" she asked.

"Nothing," said Sarah.

"Do you have something hard to do for tomorrow?"

Sarah looked down. "I have to bring in something to share with the class."

"Well, what's so hard about that? There must be something you can share with them."

"There's nothing. I have nothing to share with them. In New York I had someone I wanted to share things with. But here I have no one at all!" Sarah started to cry.

Her mother put her arms around her. "I know, baby, I know. I know just how you feel. But there has to be something about New York you might want to tell them."

"No. Nothing," Sarah cried. Out of the corner of her eye, she could see the raccoons looking at her with their surprised look. She half smiled through her tears.

"The raccoons are smiling at you, Sarah," said her mother. "They know you will come up with something." She hugged Sarah close. "Now, come on in. Those raccoons are not the only ones around here who need to be fed."

CHAPTER 8

Seeing the raccoons had made Sarah feel better. And knowing that she would feed them again tomorrow gave her something to look forward to.

After they went inside, she and her mother sat in the kitchen. It was right before dinner, but her mother decided that they should each have a slice of apple pie. Her mother was like that sometimes.

They talked while they ate the pie. Sarah told her mother about the kids at school. "Why do they say I'm stuck-up, Mom? I'm really not!"

"I know," answered her mother. "You're just quiet and rather shy. Maybe that's why they think you're stuck-up."

Sarah thought about that all evening long. She was still thinking about it when she went to bed. Maybe it was true. Maybe the kids in school were just as afraid of her as she was of them. Maybe they were like the raccoons. If you were friendly to them, maybe they would be friendly back.

Suddenly Sarah wanted to share something special with her class. But what could she share? Maybe she could talk about the merry-go-round in Central Park. But that seemed silly. After all, they had live horses here.

Sarah thought some more. She could talk about her apartment in New York. She could tell the kids how surprised she had been when her yellow curtains fitted the windows of her room in Maine. But no, that seemed silly too.

"I know!" she said aloud. She sat straight up in bed. "I'll tell about feeding the raccoons."

CHAPTER 9

The next morning, Sarah ran to school. She felt happy. She had something to share with the class.

When Sarah walked into the classroom, Julie looked at her. Instead of looking away, Sarah smiled at her. To her surprise, Julie smiled back.

Sarah sat down. Two boys went up to Julie, and they all started laughing together. But this time Sarah didn't think they were laughing at her.

A boy with red hair raised his hand.

"Billy," said the teacher, "what have you brought to show us?"

"I have this picture," Billy said. He passed around a color photograph.

When the picture got to Sarah, she jumped. There was Billy, surrounded by about thirteen raccoons. Sarah couldn't believe it. Now she had nothing to share with the class.

"In the beginning, only a few raccoons came," Billy was saying. "But then there were more and more. They kept on coming. Soon they began bringing their children. We had to give them more and more food."

All of a sudden, Sarah spoke up. "Did they ever bite you?" she asked.

Billy looked at her, surprised. "Once — when

I didn't have anything to feed them."

"What do you feed them?" asked Sarah. She was surprised to be asking so many questions.

"Oh, everything — potato peels and orange rinds and old bread. They like everything." Billy looked at her shyly. "Last week I made them a cake."

"You did?" Sarah cried.

Billy's eyes were shining. "Yes. I put in cornmeal and bacon fat and apples and some chocolate."

"Did they like it?" asked Sarah.

"They loved it. They ate every crumb. I'm going to make them another one this week."

Sarah smiled at him. "That sounds terrific," she said.

"You can come and watch," he said. "You can help me feed them."

"I'd love to," said Sarah. "You see, I asked you all those questions because we have raccoons at our house too."

"How many do you have?" asked Billy.

"Only four."

"Well, there will be more if you keep on feeding them. You'll see."

"Sarah," said the teacher, "tell us something about New York. I'm sure everyone would love to hear you talk about it."

"Yes, tell us," said Julie. "Tell us about New York."

CHAPTER 10

Sarah put her hand to her face. "I . . . I don't know what to say," she stammered.

Then she noticed her charm bracelet hanging from her wrist. "I know!" she said. "I can tell you about the Statue of Liberty. Look — this is it!" She took off the bracelet and passed it around the room.

The kids had lots of questions. "How big is

it?" "What did you do there?" "How do you get to the top?" "What can you see from up there?" "Can you see all the way to Maine?"

Sarah tried to answer all the questions. "I'm not sure what you can see from the top because I never got there. I was too scared to climb all the way up. I only got halfway."

Everybody laughed. This time Sarah laughed too. "But the worst part was going down. It took me forever. I was so scared."

"I know how you felt," said Jake. "I feel that way when I look down a thunder hole."

"A what?" asked Sarah.

"It's a hole that goes way down under the rocks. The water rushes in and out and makes a sound like thunder."

"Is there one around here?" Sarah asked.

"Yes. I could take you to see it," said Julie.

"Maybe we could all go to New York someday," Sarah said shyly. "I could show you around."

"Could you take us to the Statue of Liberty?" asked Billy.

"Yes. And . . . the merry-go-round in Central Park. I went there on my last day."

"Were you sorry to leave?" asked Julie.

"Oh, yes. Most of all I was sorry to leave my best friend."

"What was her name?"

"Susan. She was the one who gave me this

bracelet." Sarah looked at her classmates and saw that they were smiling. It was clear that they wanted to hear more. And Sarah knew she had a lot more that she wanted to tell them.

That night Sarah wrote Susan a letter.

Dear Susan,

I read your letter at least six times. I really miss you. It was so hard for me here at first. All I wanted was to go back home to New York. But now I like it better.

Maine is beautiful. Today I saw a deer. She stood still, then ran away. She looked like you when you run.

Raccoons have started coming to our house at night. You would love them. They are so funny. A boy in my class bakes special cakes for them.

On Saturday I'm going down to the ocean with a girl named Julie. She promised to show me a thunder hole. I'll write you all about it.

I've been thinking. Maybe you could come up and visit me this summer. We could go swimming. And we could feed the raccoons. Please come, Susan. Maine is not so far away!

Love and kisses,

Sarah